The Little Moon Princess

Written and illustrated by YJ LEE

HARPER

An Imprint of HarperCollinsPublishers

LONG AGO, before there were stars in the sky, a lone sparrow flew
through the dark night toward a bright light that glowed in the distance.

As the sparrow drew closer, he saw that the light was coming from a field
of flowers. In the center of each flower was a sparkling jewel. And standing
alone in the field was a little princess.

"Hello!" called the little princess, waving
to the sparrow. "Over here."

"Welcome to my moon," said the little princess with a curtsy.

The sparrow bowed and looked about. "How wonderful to have all these

beautiful jewels," he said.

"Yes," said the princess. "I love to play with my jewels, and I am very

happy living here. . . ."

". . . But when I look out beyond my moon, I can't see what's out there in the blackness. And even though I'm a princess, I still get scared. The darkness is so wide and I am so very small."

The sparrow tilted his head and looked up at the princess.
"Why don't we spread your jewels throughout the sky so they
shine in the darkness? Then you will never be afraid again."

So the princess and the sparrow plucked the gems one by one and threw them far into the deep, dark sky.

Then the sparrow took jewels in his beak and flew as far away as he could. But he soon grew tired, and most of the jewels stayed clustered close to the moon. The dark sky spread out much farther.

Next, the little princess tried to blow the jewels away, but they drifted only a short distance.

Then the little princess took off her cape and waved it up and down.
As it billowed in the air, the jewels began to scatter and spread.

The jewels floated through space and
filled even the darkest corner of the sky
with beaming points of light.

"See how they sparkle?" said the princess. "But look!
There's still one empty spot, right in the center of the sky."

So the little princess reached up and took her favorite jewel,
the one she wore in her crown, and handed it to the sparrow.

The sparrow flew all the way to the distant patch of darkness. The jewel would become the brightest star of all.

As the sparrow returned to the princess, stardust drifted from his wings and trailed behind him, forming the great Milky Way.

Now when the little princess looked out into the night sky and saw all the stars shining back at her, she knew she would never be afraid again.

Tired after their hard work, the two new friends snuggled
together and fell asleep. But first the princess tugged at
a little corner of the sky and brought some of her jewels
close to her heart.

"Good night, princess," said the sparrow.
"Good night, sparrow," said the princess.

At night, when you look up at the sky
and see the stars, remember the little
moon princess who gave up her jewels
so the night sky could sparkle and shine.

For Mom and Dad

Special thanks to Pat Cummings, Martha Rago, Maria Modugno,

Frank Olinsky, Marshall Arisman, and Carl Nicholas Titolo

Library of Congress Cataloging-in-Publication Data Lee, Y. J. The little moon princess / written and illustrated by Y.J. Lee. — 1st ed.   p.   cm.

Summary: With the help of a friendly sparrow, the little moon princess, who is afraid of the dark, uses the jewels on the surface of her moon to light up the sky.

ISBN 978-0-06-154736-2 (trade bdg.) ISBN 978-0-06-154737-9 (lib. bdg.)

[1. Princesses—Fiction. 2. Sparrows—Fiction. 3. Stars—Fiction.] I. Title. PZ7.L51518Li 2010   [E]—dc22   2009009294   CIP   AC

Typography by Martha Rago

10 11 12 13 14 SCP 10 9 8 7 6 5 4 3 2 1 ❖ First Edition

DATE DUE

JUL 1 4 2010	
JUL 2 7 2010	
JUL 2 8 2010	
SEP 1 4 2010	
OCT 1 6 2010	
NOV 3 0 2010	
DEC 0 7 2010	
APR 0 5 2011	
MAR 0 7 2014	
SEP 0 2 2014	
OCT 2 0 2014	
DEC 3 0 2014	
MAR 1 9 2015	
MAY 0 7 2015	